W9-AOF-117

Maybe Yes,
Maybe No,
Maybe Maybe

A Richard Jackson Book

ALSO BY SUSAN PATRON

Burgoo Stew

Five Bad Boys, Billy Que,
   and the Dustdobbin

Maybe Yes,
Maybe No,
Maybe Maybe

by Susan Patron

pictures by Dorothy Donahue

Orchard Books   New York

Text copyright © 1993 by Susan Patron
Illustrations copyright © 1993 by Dorothy Donahue

Orchard Books, 95 Madison Avenue, New York, NY 10016

Manufactured in the United States of America
Book design by Mina Greenstein
The text of this book is set in 15 point Goudy Old Style.
The illustrations are pencil and wash drawings reproduced in halftone.
10 9 8 7 6 5 4 3 2 1

Library of Congress Cataloging-in-Publication Data
Patron, Susan.
Maybe yes, maybe no, maybe maybe / by Susan Patron ; pictures by
Dorothy Donahue.   p.   cm. "A Richard Jackson book"—Half-title.
Summary: When her hardworking mother decides to move, eight-
year-old PK uses her imagination and storytelling to help her older
and younger sisters adjust.
ISBN 0-531-05482-9.   ISBN 0-531-08632-1 (lib. bdg.)
[1. Moving, Household—Fiction.   2. Sisters—Fiction.
3. Mothers and daughters—Fiction.]   I. Donahue, Dorothy, ill.
II. Title.   PZ7.P27565May 1993 [Fic]—dc20 92-34067

To my two best friends,
Patricia Hall Leavengood
and Georgia Lee Hall Chun

1

Billions of Stories

REAL LIFE seemed just out of PK's reach. Whenever she thought she finally understood it, everything changed and she had to start figuring it out all over again.

For instance, during the summer that PK was waiting to turn nine, both her sisters suddenly started growing up and acting different. PK, as far as she could tell, stayed exactly her same old self—and wished everyone else would, too. Instead there were hormones and weird pancakes and the riddle of the universe. Then Mama decided that the family should move. The idea of leaving their small, cozy apartment, with its built-in secret, was almost more than PK could bear.

Back when life was still more or less normal, Mama went to work every night after dinner. She was a waitress at a fancy restaurant called The Fancy Restaurant. PK and her sisters stayed home and did *their* jobs. Megan was the oldest; she washed the dishes. Next came PK, whose jobs were to answer all of Rabbit's questions and give her a bath. Rabbit's job was to get clean.

PK took her jobs seriously, which meant she spent almost her whole life doing them. It took a lot of time and energy to make up answers to all of Rabbit's questions. But PK felt that an interesting made-up answer (if she didn't know the actual answer) was much better than no answer at all.

Plus, it took hours to give Rabbit her bath.

PK always filled the tub exactly to the level of the rust stain and added bubble bath while the water was running. The pink powder burst into bubbles, like magic.

Every night, Rabbit sat in the warm water and said, "PK, tell me a story."

PK sat on the lid of the toilet. She put her arms around her knees. She curled her toes up. She thought hard.

"Give me time," PK said, concentrating.

"Okay," said Rabbit. She carefully held one corner of her washrag out of the soapy water. She sucked on that corner.

The stories came from the built-in laundry hamper across from the toilet. Billions of stories were in there.

Every night, PK found a different one.

"Princess Rabba was the youngest of three sisters," PK began.

"Wait," said Rabbit. "Megan isn't here yet. She has to be here before you start the story."

Until recently, Megan had always hoisted herself up on the sink and stared at herself in the medicine cabinet mirror during PK's hamper stories.

PK said, "She finished the dishes. If she wanted to be here, she would be here. Maybe Megan has gotten too grown-up for hamper stories."

"*I* will never be too grown-up for them," said Rabbit. "Okay. Go ahead."

PK continued, "No one thinks Princess Rabba can do anything because she is so small. But Princess Rabba has many amazing adventures. One day she discovered the terrible secret of why there is a pouf of dust when a peanut shell is cracked open. . . ."

As PK told the story, Rabbit's eyes glazed over. She forgot to suck her washrag. She forgot she was taking a bath. She just sat still in the water and listened.

At the end of the story, Rabbit asked, "PK, did you make that up?"

4 ·   "No, Rabbit," said PK. "I found it in the laundry hamper, like the other stories."

Rabbit frowned. "Today I looked in the laundry hamper," she said. "I took out all the dirty clothes and looked in all the corners. But I couldn't find any stories. Then I even sat on the toilet lid just like you do. I put my feet on the edge and curled my toes up. I made my brain wait a long time. I *still* couldn't find any stories."

"Well, those stories are in there, all right," said PK. "Did you smell anything?"

"Yes," said Rabbit. "I did."

"It was stories you smelled. They rub off people's skin. Those stories rub off onto sheets and shirts and jeans. So stories smell like people. And that's the proof that they are in the hamper." PK shrugged and fluttered her bangs by blowing air up under them. "It is not something I can show you how, Rabbit. It is just a kind of magic in that hamper."

But deep inside, PK worried that the hamper magic would someday disappear, just like the bubbles in Rabbit's bath.

2

Human Jam

RABBIT HAD BEEN in the bathtub for so long (because the hamper story that night took a long time to tell) that her fingers got good and wrinkled. To PK, this meant Rabbit was clean enough.

"You can get out now," PK said. "And tomorrow we will find out that Princess Rabba's mother has been looking in the want ads for a new castle. Pretty soon, Princess Rabba and the royal family are going to have to move."

"I am not really clean enough yet," said · 7 Rabbit. "Tell about it now."

PK laughed. "Nope," she said. "The next hamper story will begin tomorrow night at bath time."

Megan opened the door and popped her head in. "What are you weenies doing? You've been in here *forever*."

"Nothing," said PK. "Giving Rabbit her bath. And we aren't weenies."

"Megan," said Rabbit, "I know why there's a pouf of dust when you crack open a peanut, but I can't tell you because it's a hamper story and only PK can tell hamper stories."

"Good for you," said Megan. "Now would you *please* hurry up in here? And *try* not to leave your weenie-clothes lying all over the floor." Megan left, closing the door. She did not see the face PK made at her.

After getting Rabbit dried off and into her nightie, PK picked up a small pair of dirty red socks. She took a sniff and smiled and threw them into the hamper. Maybe they were weenie-clothes, but one thing PK knew for sure: they were loaded with stories.

PK was the sister in the middle. There was one sister before her and one sister after. One above and one below. No matter what she did, she would always be stuck between them, right in the middle.

Another of PK's jobs, which was nearly as hard as answering all of Rabbit's questions, was trying to stay friends with Megan. Megan was very pretty and almost-a-teenager. Also, she was Gifted. PK figured that Gifted meant using big words regular people did not understand.

Megan had all sorts of rules and codes. Sometimes she meditated, which meant everyone else had to be absolutely silent. No one could talk to her or look at her. Sometimes Megan worked on her image. This meant she took all her clothes and Mama's old hats and scarves and purses into the bathroom and locked the door. Megan's image

was that she was different from other kids. She hated being like everyone else. The absolute worst insult Megan could give was, "You're just like everyone else."

Megan often told PK she was just like everyone else.

PK tried hard not to be, but sometimes she couldn't help it.

THAT NIGHT, after Mama had gone to work and after Rabbit's bath, PK lay on her bed, doing her homework for summer school.

Rabbit, sitting in a nest of Barbie doll clothes near her rollaway bed, asked, "PK, how much longer is it until kindergarten?"

"I'm doing my homework. Four weeks," said PK.

"You're just like everyone else, PK," said Megan from her bunk. "*Everyone* does their homework at night before bed."

"When else is there to do it?" asked PK. She spoke to the bottoms of Megan's feet, which were dangling over the side of the top bunk. Like everything about Megan, the soles of her feet were beautiful.

Megan sighed loudly. PK knew without being able to see that Megan had rolled up her eyes in her head. That was her way of letting PK know it was a dumb question.

"Yeah," said Rabbit. "When else?"

"There's the middle of the night, for one thing," said Megan. "Have you ever even *tried* getting up at midnight, PK, when the world slumbers, with only yourself for company? Of course not," she said, answering her own question. "All you ever do is sleep, which is so boring. You have no idea what you are missing."

PK thought Mama would not be too happy about her getting up at midnight to do her homework.

"What if you're too *asleep* to do your homework in the middle of the night?" asked Rabbit worriedly.

12 ·

"Or four o'clock in the morning," Megan said to PK, ignoring Rabbit. "Getting up at four, before dawn, is incredible. Artists always work in the early morning. That is when brilliant ideas are most often born."

Megan knew about things like when brilliant ideas are born because of being Gifted. Megan had lots of brilliant ideas. The only ideas PK ever had were normal, just-like-everyone-else ideas.

"Take me, for instance," said Megan. "I am currently struggling to establish my intellectual and moral independence from Mama. Do you think I can do that by *sleeping*? Certainly not."

"How *do* you establish your intellectual and moral independence from Mama?" asked PK. It sounded as if Megan might be planning to get a job as a brain surgeon.

"Yeah," said Rabbit. "How do you?"

"You bedbrains wouldn't understand," said Megan. "Your Life Experience has been pitifully meager."

This was what she always said when conversations got interesting.

PK thought of her pitifully meager Life Experience. She supposed that the only actual Life Experience she had had was being born, which she couldn't even remember. Aside from that one event, she had lived her life squeezed between her two sisters like the inside of a sticky sandwich. On one side was Rabbit, worried about kindergarten and homework. On the other side was Megan, with her perfect toes and her brilliant ideas. Rabbit, stubborn and worried. Megan, stubborn and perfect. And there was PK herself, kind of a human jam, stuck forever in the middle.

3

Megan

"MAMA, WHAT A splendid and elegant repast," Megan said the next night after dinner, meaning she liked it. Dinner was homemade spaghetti, garlic toast, and Popsicles.

Before she became almost-a-teenager, Megan used to play with PK and Rabbit. She always perched on the sink and looked at herself close up in the mirror. She always listened to the hamper stories.

Then Megan got strange. She quit hanging

around with PK and Rabbit. "I don't associate with babies" was her Gifted way of putting it. "And no touching my things. No listening when I talk on the phone. No long baths when I need the bathroom."

PK could hardly stand it anymore. So when Megan called the spaghetti dinner a splendid and elegant repast, PK leaned over at the waist and pretended she was gagging. She couldn't help it.

"You doorknob," said Megan, and went into the living room. PK heard her fling herself into the big blue chair.

Mama shook her head. "Good thing that big blue chair is so sturdy," she said. "You girls seem to fling yourselves into it on a regular basis."

"That's what it's *for*," said PK. She thought a minute. "Mama?" she said. "What's wrong with Megan?"

Mama was about to leave for work. She rummaged in her purse to make sure her apartment key was in it. She said, "Megan is growing up.

16 ·

She's almost-a-teenager. It's hormones that make her act like that."

PK wished Megan would grow down instead of up. Then things would be the way they used to be.

Mama was hurrying so she wouldn't be late. She flew out of the apartment with her special shoes and her fancy waitress uniform in a tote bag, calling out reminders to be good and not to stay up too late. PK locked the door behind her.

PK walked in a normal way into the living room. Then she turned her back to the big blue chair and walked sideways, like a crab, so she wouldn't have to look at Megan. She went into the bedroom, where Rabbit was picking out her bedtime story from a pile of library books. She told Rabbit, "Megan has hormones because she is almost-a-teenager. That's why she acts strange." PK added, "Time for your bath."

Rabbit said, "Is Princess Rabba going to move in the hamper story tonight?"

18 ·

"You'll see."

"Poor Princess Rabba. She hates moving, doesn't she, PK?"

"Well, she hates packing," said PK.

"PK, when you are almost-a-teenager, will you have hormones?"

"Yes," said PK sadly.

"But will you act mean, like Megan?"

PK did not know. "Maybe yes," she said. "Maybe no. . . ." She shrugged. "Maybe maybe." But she certainly hoped not.

4

Bike

AFTER SUMMER SCHOOL the next day, PK went for a ride on her bike, who was named Bike. Bike had been upset lately.

PK rode until she found a private place. She sat on the grass and made Bike lie down next to her. She put her hand on the rear tire.

"Don't be sad, Bike," PK said. "Deep down, Megan is still Megan. But now she has hormones and can't act normal."

Bike listened.

"Mama's hunting for a better building to live in. Even though we hate moving, I bet Megan will get nicer afterward. Try not to be so worried," said PK.

Bike felt a little better.

"Mama's really busy working and apartment hunting. Megan's busy being almost-a-teenager. They're just too busy for Rabbit and me right now."

Bike knew this was true.

"Another thing," said PK. "I've noticed Rabbit is leaving a lot of old carrot stubs around, with little grooves in them. You know what *that* means. It means Rabbit is scraping with her bottom teeth, which she does when things are not okay. Maybe she's worried about moving or about going to kindergarten. So I will try to pay more attention to her."

After a while, PK said, "Do you feel better now, Bike?"

Bike did.

"Good," said PK, and rode home.

5

Rabbit

As soon as PK got home, Rabbit started asking questions.

"Do people call me Rabbit because I love carrots?" she asked.

"No," said PK. "When you were a baby, you hated carrots."

"That's because baby-food carrots aren't *real* carrots. They're cooked and mashed. They're yucky."

"Don't you remember the story of why you are called Rabbit?"

"Yes," said Rabbit. "But I want you to tell it again."

"Your real name is Rebecca," PK began. "When you started to learn to talk, I tried to teach you to say your name. You could only say Rabba. You were such a cute baby that people would come right up to us and say, 'What's your name, cutie pie?' and you would answer, 'Rabba.' Then Mama would explain, 'She can't say Rebecca, so she says Rabba.' "

"Was I cuter than you when you were a baby?" asked Rabbit.

"No," said PK. "Mama says we were all equally cute."

"Was I the smartest?"

"No, we were all equally smart."

"Megan says she was the cutest *and* the smartest. She knew twenty-one nursery rhymes by heart before she was two years old."

PK sighed. Megan was always better at everything. She was even better at being a baby. "I know," she said. "But since you were the young-est, you had to be the most stubborn!"

"How stubborn was I?"

"Well," PK said, "one day a lady asked you what your name was, and you said, 'I can't say Rebecca, so I say Rabba.' "

"I love this part," said Rabbit.

"I know," said PK. "Anyway, everyone laughed, but you were serious. You kept insisting, 'I can't say Rebecca, so I say Rabba.' So we all called you Rabba until you discovered how much you loved carrots. Then you just became Rabbit."

"Will the kids in kindergarten tease me about being called Rabbit?"

"Yes," said PK, nodding. "Especially if you keep five or six carrot sticks in every one of your pockets, as usual."

"PK, what should I say when the kindergarten kids tease me?"

PK thought that over. "Just say whatever you
26 · think Princess Rabba would say," she answered

after a while. "Remember, even though Princess Rabba is small, she's very stubborn and very smart."

"Just like me," said Rabbit, and PK smiled.

6

Carrots and Pancakes

"PLEASE SCRAPE ME A CARROT," Rabbit said to Megan the next morning.

"I am extremely busy," said Megan, leaning over a thick book and stirring pancake batter. "Scrape your own carrot." She was reading and making breakfast at the same time.

Rabbit began to cry. "Mama said I'm too young to scrape carrots," she said.

"Shhh," said PK. "We can't wake up Mama."

28 · Mama always slept late in the morning because

she worked the night shift at The Fancy Restaurant.

PK put her glass on top of the comics section of the newspaper to show that she wasn't finished reading it and that no one else should take it. "I'll scrape your carrot. But listen: if you ever need a carrot badly and there's no one to scrape it, here's what you do. Take the carrot out of the fridge. Climb up to the sink and turn on the water. Scrub the carrot all over to get off the dirt. Then eat it."

"I hate carrots when they're not scraped," said Rabbit. "I do not like it when there is a green thing at one end and a thin tail at the other end. The ends must be cut off for it to be a good carrot."

PK thought of her talk with Bike. "Okay," she said. "I will always scrape your carrot for you. I will always cut off the green thing at one end and the thin tail at the other end."

30 ·   "I love you, PK," said Rabbit. "I'm glad you don't have hormones."

"Me too," said PK. "Now go get dressed for day care *quietly*. And when you come back, the pancakes will be ready."

Rabbit tiptoed to the bedroom, crunching her carrot. PK went back to the comics.

"Fascinating," said Megan.

PK looked up. "What's fascinating?" she asked.

Megan acted surprised that PK was sitting there. "Oh, nothing. Just talking to myself." She smiled a secret little smile.

This made PK curious. "What is so fascinating about pancake batter?" she asked.

"Oh, you wouldn't understand," said Megan.

Nothing made PK madder than those words. But she had learned that Megan *liked* to get her mad, so she pretended she was not interested. She shrugged her shoulders. She read the comics.

"It's wonderful to be almost-a-teenager," said Megan.

"Why?" asked PK before she could stop herself from getting interested again.

"Because of the fascinating things you learn in school about becoming a woman," said Megan.

"Like what?"

Megan smiled her secret little smile again. PK felt like bashing her head in, only she knew that would get her nowhere. She sighed. "Megan, tell me or don't tell me, but hurry up so I can finish reading the comics."

"Well," said Megan. "We saw this movie. It was about becoming a woman."

"Yeah?" One part of PK wanted to know this stuff. Another part did *not* want to know it.

"In the movie, three girls are spending the night together. One girl's mom is a nurse, and they're at that girl's house. So the nurse-mom explains to them about becoming a woman."

"Yeah?" said PK.

"Okay, so the nurse-mom is making pancakes, right? So she makes a pancake in the shape of a uterus!" Megan burst out laughing.

"In the shape of a what?" asked PK.

"A uterus," said Megan. "The organ inside women where babies grow." Megan acted as if *everybody* knew the word "uterus."

"Then what happened?" asked PK.

"It is not a question of what *happened*," said Megan. "That was it, basically. Come here and I'll show you."

PK thought it sounded like a dumb movie. She went over to the stove. Megan poured the batter into the pan in a certain way. The pancake was shaped kind of like a pear. Megan burst out laughing again.

It was not very funny, but PK laughed, too. She laughed to pretend that she understood why the pear-shaped blob was funny. She laughed to pretend it didn't matter that Megan was becoming a woman.

But PK no longer wanted pancakes for breakfast.

7

The Riddle of the Universe

MAMA HAD BEEN apartment hunting all week, checking out places advertised in the *Los Angeles Times.* Now she was in the living room, packing books in cardboard boxes. She was determined to find a new apartment soon, so they could move before school began in the fall.

PK trudged in and flung herself into the big blue chair. Mama stopped packing books. She put her hands on her hips.

"PK, what is the matter?" asked Mama.

"I hate having to pack, I hate having to move, and I *hate* being the middle sister."

"I see," said Mama.

"And Megan and Rabbit are growing up instead of down."

Mama nodded understandingly. "True," she said.

"It's so unfair! No matter how hard I try, I'm never as smart as Megan. I'm never as pretty. And I'm *never* as grown-up." Two big tears slid out of PK's eyes.

"Mmm," said Mama. "What else?"

"I've taught Rabbit everything I know so far. But there's a lot of stuff I don't know," PK sobbed. "My only true friend in the whole world is Bike!"

Mama laughed. She sat down on the wide arm of the blue chair. She took PK's wet face between her two hands. "You have drama in your blood, PK. You must find good ways to use such talent."

PK looked into her mother's eyes to see if she was teasing. Mama was smiling, but she was serious.

"I have drama in my blood?" PK asked. Mama nodded. PK could almost feel that drama in her blood, zinging through her body.

Mama said, "Megan will always have to work hard in life. First, because she is the oldest child, so she has no one to learn from, like you and Rabbit do. And second, because she's gifted. People always expect more from her."

PK knew this was true. Megan's teachers always wanted more from her than from other kids.

"And Rabbit," Mama went on, "little Rabbit has fortitude! She knows exactly what she wants, but she usually has to fight to get it. At the same time, she's a truly sweet child. Having you and Megan as sisters is both wonderful and very, very hard for her."

"What about me, Mama? I'm not like Megan or Rabbit, am I?"

"No, PK. You are the dreamer and storyteller. You always go around with your nose in the clouds. And you are lucky there is a sister on each side to grab hold of when you trip and stumble on a dream."

Tripping on a dream was an idea that made PK smile. She looked at her big toes. There was a Band-Aid on one. The other was scraped. So maybe it was true. Maybe the reason she stubbed her toes so often was all that drama zinging in her blood, and all those stories and dreams in her head.

"One thing that's very strange, PK," said Mama, "but somehow comforting: the universe always unfolds exactly as it was meant to. Do you understand that?" Mama brushed PK's bangs to the side, as if by doing that she could see right into PK's mind.

PK thought about the universe unfolding exactly as it was meant to. It seemed almost like a riddle. "Yes, Mama," she said at last. "It means I should be glad I'm the middle sister, right?"

"Right," said Mama.

8

Cherry Pits
and Plastic Ants

PACKING WAS EVEN WORSE than PK had expected, since Mama had asked her to sort through her collections and throw away things she no longer wanted. There was *nothing* she no longer wanted.

PK collected small boxes and writing paper and shells and buttons and pennies. She collected labels from packages of spaghetti and old bottle caps. She couldn't imagine throwing out any of her collections, especially not the best ones: her cherry pit collection and her tiny plastic glow-in-the-dark insects.

PK had thousands of cherry pits. They filled up three and a half shoe boxes. Every year Mama took the girls to a special farm where they climbed up in the trees and picked the cherries themselves. It was fun, it did not cost much, and they could eat all the cherries they wanted. PK saved every cherry pit.

Mama came into the bedroom and sat down on Rabbit's rollaway bed. She watched as PK carefully taped shut her boxes of cherry pits.

"PK, why do you save cherry pits?" Mama asked.

"They are good for making beanbags, I think," said PK. "Also, foot warmers. See, you heat the pits in the oven. They stay hot a long time. You fill up a cloth sack with them, and you put the sack at the foot of your bed, under the covers."

"But PK, it doesn't get that cold in Los Angeles. We don't need foot warmers here. And what would you do with a beanbag?"

PK breathed deeply. It is hard for people who

collect things to explain why to people who do not collect things. PK had tried explaining over and over to Megan, who yelped, "Cherry pits! That is *disgusting!*" To her, PK's stuff was just junk. It took up a lot of space, and it was all over the bedroom.

"Mama," PK said, pulling open a box she had just taped shut, "just stick your hand in this shoe box. Just feel these cherry pits." PK loved the cherry pits in and of themselves. They didn't have to have a purpose to be valuable to her.

Mama stuck her hand in the box of cherry pits, which were smooth and hard and round. PK had scrubbed them until they were very clean. She had dried them in the sun. Mama smiled.

"So really," she said, "you collect these because they *feel* good."

PK shrugged. That was part of it.

Finally, Mama gave up. "Okay," she said. "But try to keep everything out of Rabbit's reach, and out of Megan's way. I just hope we can afford

42 ·

a bigger apartment. We're going to need it with all these collections."

PK sighed. Her whole life seemed to consist of keeping things out of Rabbit's reach and out of Megan's way—even though her plastic glow-in-the-dark insect collection hardly took up any space at all. She kept her ants, cockroaches, and flies in three separate small boxes from her box collection. She loved to think of them glowing brightly inside their boxes.

But her real plan, when she finally collected enough of them, was to glue the ants to the wall by her bed. They would be crawling in a long line, just like real ants. The line would go up to the ceiling. If she had lots and lots of ants, the line would go *across* the ceiling.

Those ants would glow in the dark and cheer her up when she was sad.

That is what a collection is for.

9
Moving

THE NEXT AFTERNOON, Mama burst into the living room, jingling a new set of keys. "Girls, guess what!" she said. "I found us a great apartment only five blocks away. It's bigger than this one. PK and Rabbit will easily be able to walk to school together when Rabbit starts kindergarten. And it's not far from Megan's new school, either."

"All I care about," said Megan, "is having my own room."

"There are two bedrooms, one for me and one

for PK and Rabbit to share. Plus there's a very small den," said Mama. "We can let Megan have the den for her room."

"How come *Megan* gets her own room?" asked PK. "I'm the one who needs space for my collections. I need a place for Bike. I need a desk where I can write down my stories."

"We'll get you some shelves for your collections, PK," said Mama. "And we'll get you a desk of your own. We'll find a place for Bike. Megan gets the den because she's almost-a-teenager. She needs more privacy now."

PK figured that this had something to do with pancake blobs. She flung herself into the big blue chair.

Rabbit said, "Mama? Is there a laundry hamper at the new apartment?"

"I didn't really notice," said Mama, "but I don't think so. Those built-in hampers are so old-fashioned. We'll get a basket hamper. All this is going to cost a lot of money." Mama frowned as · 45

she spoke. PK knew that meant more bills to pay.

Rabbit flung herself into the big blue chair next to PK. She got a carrot out of her pocket and began to gnaw a groove in it with her bottom teeth.

PK thought, More bills. No hamper full of stories to tell Rabbit. Megan in her own room, doing secret, private, almost-a-teenager things. Having to explain your collections. And packing, packing, packing.

If it were up to me, she thought, there would be a law against moving when someone's life is in the middle of changing. Moving should happen only when everything else is normal. And people should never have to move away from the world's only laundry hamper full of stories.

10

A Secret Message

PK WENT OUT to ride Bike. She rode around and around. "Bike, oh, Bike," she said. "If there's no built-in hamper, I may not be able to find any more stories for Rabbit. She'll never want to take her bath. She won't get clean. There will be no Princess Rabba stories to explain things. Rabbit will be so sad."

She cried as she thought of poor, poor Rabbit, with no more stories. There were too many changes going on. PK hated having so many changes at once.

Even Bike looked sad. "Poor, poor Bike," she sobbed.

PK rode back home. She went into the bathroom and shut the door. At least the hamper will always be here, she thought. Even though we move away, the hamper will stay. And whenever anyone throws dirty clothes in it, they will also be throwing in stories. Too bad the new people moving in won't know the secret treasure of this hamper. Or the people who move in after *them*. Or the people who move in centuries and centuries from now.

She pulled up the silver ring handle of the hamper. She lifted the heavy lid all the way up and leaned it back against the wall. Then PK got a felt-tip marker. Very carefully, in tiny letters, she wrote something on the edge of the side of the lid.

She wrote:

THERE IS A SECRET IN HERE.

Beside that, she put:

PK

PK hoped that in a hundred years someone would find her message and figure out the secret. It would have to be someone whose blood was zinging with drama—someone who could smell the stories in a dirty sock. Because it would be tragic for all those good stories to go to waste.

11

A Giant
Redwood

PK AND RABBIT were packing their clothes in
cardboard boxes from the supermarket. Rabbit
was carefully folding her Barbie's clothes.

"Are bats the only mammals that fly?" Rabbit
asked.

PK had taught Rabbit everything she knew,
especially about bats and redwoods and dinosaurs.
Rabbit loved bats and redwoods and dinosaurs.
So when PK ran out of true facts, she made up
stuff about them.

"Yes," said PK, though she was not at all sure this was true. "Because bats were the only animals smart enough to ask the birds to teach them." She blew air up on her forehead.

"PK, how do you make your bangs flutter like that?"

PK explained, "You stick your lower lip out. You blow hard. You force the air up." But no matter how hard Rabbit tried, she couldn't blow the air up. She could not flutter her bangs.

PK tried to get Rabbit to be patient. She knew that the harder Rabbit tried, the more frustrated she got. "Rabbit, think of a giant redwood," said PK. "It grows slowly, but it's very strong. The wind flutters its leaves when the wind is ready. And you will flutter your bangs when you are ready." PK didn't really expect her sister to be patient. She knew Rabbit could hardly stand waiting for something this important.

"I am ready! I am ready now!" said Rabbit. "I already have six things to ask my teacher on the

first day of school. I better not ask her to teach me how to flutter my bangs, too. Maybe she'll think I ask too many questions." Rabbit got a carrot out of her pocket. She gnawed on it with her bottom teeth.

"Don't be so worried about kindergarten," said PK. "You will do fine."

"What if the teacher finds out I only pretend to take naps? What if she looks at my eyes and can tell I am not really asleep?"

"You won't get in trouble for not falling asleep, as long as you *pretend* to be asleep," said PK. PK herself had gone all through kindergarten pretending to take a nap every day. It was very boring. "Try telling stories to yourself while you pretend to be asleep," she said.

Rabbit looked sad. "I can't tell stories to myself," she said. "I don't know how. Maybe at nap time, you could come into my kindergarten room and whisper stories to me while the other children are sleeping."

"No," said PK. "They wouldn't let me out of my own room for that. But everything will be okay. You'll see. . . . By the way, Rabbit," PK added, "I bet you will be able to flutter your bangs as soon as you stop worrying. And you will probably turn out to be the best bang-flutterer in the family." Since PK considered herself to be a first-class bang-flutterer, it was generous of her to say so.

And it was a good thing, a lucky thing, PK realized, that Megan had long hair, parted in the middle—with no bangs at all.

12
The Big Blue Chair

MAMA, MEGAN, PK, and Rabbit sat on cartons of books in the middle of the living room, passing around a carton of popcorn. As soon as Aunt Angela and Uncle Jack arrived, everyone would start carrying things down for loading in Jack's pickup truck. PK looked around the living room, realizing it was probably her last look at the place she had lived in most of her life. She knew the apartment would miss her dreadfully. Already it looked gray and abandoned.

She was glad they would have their old, familiar furniture at the new apartment. "Where are we going to put the big blue chair?" she asked.

"We're not taking the big blue chair to the new apartment," Mama said.

Megan and PK looked at each other, shocked. "But Mama," said Megan. "We've always had the big blue chair. You nursed Rabbit in that chair. PK learned her right from her left by pinning a safety pin on one of its arms, remember? I taught myself to read *Hop on Pop* in it. That chair is like a member of the family!"

"It is!" said PK. "For a lot of people, this chair would be just like their dog." It had never before occurred to PK how much the big blue chair was like a faithful dog that she had known and loved all her life.

Mama looked at the big blue chair. "Sorry, girls, but this chair is too old. We've flung ourselves into it so much that it's worn out. And it's just too *big*. Besides, we're getting Aunt Angela's almost-new Hide-A-Bed couch. One part of mov-

ing is letting go of things you don't really need anymore. That way, you get a whole new fresh start on life."

"What will happen to our chair then?" asked Megan.

A horrible thought struck PK. She walked over and stroked the faded blue fabric as if it were the fur of a dog. "Will it be put to sleep?" she whispered.

"PK, honestly," Mama said, laughing. "It's a *chair*. We'll give it to Goodwill."

"This is not funny, Mama," said PK. "This is serious."

For maybe the last time ever, PK flung herself into the big blue chair, her dear old friend. She cleared her throat. "This chair has held us during our happy times and during our sad times," she said, sitting up straight, as if she were the President of the United States, making a speech on TV. "It has always been part of our lives. To us,

it is a historic chair and a faithful friend."

"Yeah," said Rabbit, who was close to tears from listening to Megan and PK.

"I'll even put it in my room if you let us keep it," Megan said.

Mama did some head rolls. She rolled her head to one side, back, and to the other side. She did this when she felt stressed out. "Megan, that's silly. That chair would take up nearly your whole room. You don't realize how really big it is. Besides, it's not a bedroom chair. It's a living room chair. And it is *not* going to the new apartment."

"Mama, *please*," said all three sisters.

"No, girls. That is final. Now give me a break and drop the subject."

Mama did some more head rolls. She looked tired.

PK thought about letting go of things. It reminded her of those stages Mama was always talking about. "It's a stage you just have to go through in order to grow up," she would say. But why do they make the stages so hard? PK wondered. It seemed a lot to ask of people. Maybe it was so that your Life Experience would no longer be so pitifully meager.

Usually Megan went through the stages first, and PK knew what was coming before she got there a couple of years later. Now Megan seemed to feel just as she did. Maybe this time, for once, PK herself would go through a stage first. She would be the first to let go, the first to get a fresh new start on life, the one to set an example.

Suddenly PK stopped needing the big blue chair, even though she still loved it and always would. Her body felt different, as if there were brand-new blood being pumped through her heart. She was positive that this meant she was actually having a Life Experience.

"Listen," she said to her sisters. "Pretend you are the new people moving in. You really didn't want to move, and you already miss your old apartment. You *hated* to move. You come in here and you find this wonderful, historic chair. You see how perfect it is in this room, right in this very spot."

Megan frowned and then nodded slowly. "PK is right, for once," she said. "The new people really need this chair. The *apartment* needs it."

"Yeah," said Rabbit, who was now feeling very sorry for the new people having to leave their old apartment. She had never even thought about *them* before. "Our old blue chair will make those poor sad people happy, won't it, PK?"

"Yes," said PK, in the firm, grown-up voice of a person who has just gone through a stage before her older sister. "Definitely."

13

A Heart like a Shredded Tire

PK DECIDED that moving was another Life Experience. She now hoped she wouldn't have *too* many Life Experiences in her life.

The worst thing that had happened was that Bike's front tire somehow got ripped. It was torn to shreds. PK did not dare ask Mama for money for a new tire. There were too many bills. And Mama was exhausted, since they had done the moving themselves, loading and unloading the pickup three times. There were still lots of unpacked boxes stacked in the new living room. So PK just leaned Bike against the wall near her new desk.

A few days later, PK went to sit next to Bike. She stroked the poor ripped tire. "Bike," she said. "There are no stories in this new apartment. It is clean and bright, and Mama and Megan love it here, but I feel all empty and strange. I miss Megan not being in the top bunk. The kitchen is not in the right place, and I still haven't found my boxes of cherry pits. Worst of all, I think that when we throw our dirty clothes in the new wicker laundry hamper, the stories *escape* through the air holes." PK tenderly fingered the torn shreds of rubber. She imagined her own heart, torn and black, hanging limply in her chest. "Bike, my heart is like your tire," she said.

Bike understood exactly how PK felt.

"I've decided to go back to the old apartment. I'll stand outside and concentrate on the hamper. Maybe there is still one little story in it, one I left

behind. I have got to find out. Since you are injured, dear Bike, I must go alone."

So PK walked sadly back to the old building.

A family was just moving in, and people were going back and forth with boxes. PK saw a boy sitting on the curb, holding a skateboard. He looked older than Rabbit but younger than PK. He saw her and smiled and raised one eyebrow way up on his forehead.

PK went over to the boy. "I used to live here long, long ago," she said. It was actually only three days since they had moved, but it felt as long ago to PK as the time of a folktale. "Those were some of the happiest days of my life."

The boy stared at her. "Are you PK?" he asked.

"Yes," said PK.

"I am Josh. I found your message."

This did not surprise PK. She now knew that the universe was unfolding exactly the way it was meant to. Meaning, people may find secret mes- · 67 sages right away instead of a hundred years later when you thought they would.

"Could I go into your bathroom for a second?" she asked. "I need to look for something I lost."

"Sure," said Josh, "if you tell me the secret of the hamper."

"Hmm," said PK. "Do you have any brothers or sisters?"

"No, I'm an only child."

"Well, it may work, or it may not. Depends. But I will tell you the secret. Let's go."

14

Josh

PK FOLLOWED JOSH into her old apartment, but at first she thought that it was the wrong place. The walls were painted the color of peaches, and lacy white curtains hung at the windows. The old apartment did not look sad and lonely, as PK had expected. It did not look as if it missed her at all. It looked happy.

The big blue chair was exactly where it had always been. PK flung herself into it for old times' sake. It felt, somehow, a bit smaller than before.

"My dad *loves* that old chair," said Josh. "He says he's going to re-cover it in an elegant dark green fabric."

PK smiled. The big blue chair was getting a fresh new start on life.

They went into the bathroom. PK pulled down the lid of the toilet and sat on it. "Okay," she said. "The secret in the hamper is stories, really good ones. Billions of them. There's a certain way to get them out. It works best if someone's taking a bath and asking lots of questions. But it *can* work if you're alone."

"So far, this is incredible," said Josh. "Elucidate further, please."

This was what Megan said when she wanted something explained.

"Are you by any chance Gifted?" PK asked.

"Yes," said Josh. "Why?"

"Nothing. I just happen to have a very Gifted sister. I am probably a bit Gifted, too, just from being around her all the time. Like the way you catch the flu."

"Cool," said Josh. "I hope some of *you* rubs off on *her,* too."

PK was pretty sure that this was a compliment. It was a weird situation that made her feel confused. She wasn't at all sure what to say. So she thought a minute and blew air on her forehead to flutter her bangs. "Maybe yes," she said, "maybe no." She shrugged. "Maybe maybe."

Then PK got down to business. "Now," she said, "here's how you get the stories. You sit here. You put your heels up on the rim—bare feet is best—and you hug your knees. You curl your toes up. You stare at that built-in hamper. The stories in it have rubbed off people onto their clothes and sheets and stuff."

PK noticed with great interest that Josh moved his eyebrows around a lot. He could move one without moving the other. PK tried doing this herself but was unable to. She had never met anyone with such athletic eyebrows.

"This is the tricky part," she continued. "You have to open a little window in your mind. A

story from the hamper will fly into your mind if the window is open. That's the only way I can explain it."

Josh said, "Let me try."

PK sat on the edge of the tub. She felt a brief sadness at the sight of the old rust stain that marked the right water level for Rabbit's bath. Never again would Rabbit have a bath in that wonderful tub.

Josh took off his thongs and sat on the toilet seat. He hugged his knees and curled his toes up. He stared at the hamper. A long time went by.

"Give me time," said Josh. He scrunched his eyebrows right down over his eyes, concentrating hard.

"Okay," said PK. More time went by.

"I think there's a story about to fly into my little window," Josh said. "But I'm pretty new at this. Maybe I need to practice."

"Too bad you don't have a little sister in the bathtub. That helps a lot," said PK. "Or an older · 73 sister who sits on the sink."

"Actually," said Josh, "I'm *glad* I don't have two sisters in the bathroom with me. Do you think I could use Slick?"

"Who's Slick?" asked PK.

Josh turned a little red. He got up and put his skateboard in the tub. "Don't laugh," he said. "Slick is my skateboard."

PK did not laugh. She raised her eyebrows delicately and smiled.

"Splendid and elegant," she said, just like a Gifted person. "I'm sure you will find stories in the hamper."

PK got up. "I have to go now," she said.

"You didn't look for the thing you lost," said Josh.

"No," said PK. "But I think I found it anyway."

15

Ants

It was Monday, Mama's night off. She stuck her head in PK and Rabbit's room. "I'll give Rabbit her bath," said Mama. "You need to start organizing your collections, PK."

"May I start gluing my ants to the wall?"

Mama had asked the new landlord if it was all right for PK to do this. "The landlord said okay," said Mama. "I couldn't believe it. But he said he remembers being your age. So go ahead with the ants." Mama paused and looked straight into PK's · 75 eyes. "But PK—no cockroaches are to be glued to the wall. That is final."

"Yes, Mama," said PK, and nodded to show that she understood about no cockroaches being glued to the wall.

Megan came in and watched for a while. It was slow work. PK wanted her ants to be in a perfect line, like real ants—a line that went straight and then zigged and zagged around things in the way.

Finally, Megan said, "PK, I have to admit something. Those ants are really cool. Gluing them to the wall makes them a work of art. I think maybe you aren't like everybody else. Maybe you are almost-an-artist."

"Well," said PK. She was pretty surprised. She thought, suddenly, of Life Experiences. For some reason, an image of the old blue chair turning into an elegant new dark green chair came into her mind.

Megan heard the phone ringing in the kitchen

and jumped up to get it. PK lay down on her bed and stared at the ceiling with her new, almost-an-artist eyes. Luckily, Mama had not mentioned anything about gluing flies. Luckily, she had not said a word about the ceiling.

16

Clean When Wrinkled

From the bedroom, PK heard Rabbit and Mama talking in the bathroom. She got up and tiptoed to the bathroom door and stood there, listening. She wanted to find out if Rabbit would say anything about missing the hamper stories.

PK was surprised to hear Rabbit say, "I *hate* taking baths."

"Rabbit! I thought you loved baths!" said Mama.

"I used to, in the old building. Now I hate ·79 them."

"Why?" Mama asked.

"I don't know," PK heard Rabbit say. "Because I'm a giant redwood. My feet are my roots. My redwood roots have sunk deep into the ground."

"Okay, but you have to take a bath anyway," said Mama. "Here's your old washrag that you like to suck. Here's some bubble bath."

PK smiled at the silence that followed. She knew Rabbit was standing there being a giant redwood tree.

Finally, Mama said, "Rebecca, why won't you get into the bathtub?"

"I need a story," Rabbit said, "so I'll know when it's time to get out."

"I don't get it," said Mama.

"When the story ends, if I'm wrinkled, it means I'm clean enough to get out."

"Then I will read you your bedtime story now," said Mama.

"No, the bedtime story is for bedtime. I need a hamper story."

"I have a feeling that only PK knows hamper stories," Mama said.

"Yes," said Rabbit. PK smiled again. "But Mama, that's not all. The worst part is that there's no built-in hamper here. Where will PK get her stories?"

"I don't know," said Mama. "I'm sure PK will figure something out. Let's ask her."

17

A Good One

"PK," Mama called. "Please come here right now."

PK waited a few minutes so that Mama and Rabbit wouldn't know she had been listening at the door. Then she went into the bathroom. Rabbit had her clothes off and was standing next to the bathtub with her arms out from her sides. Rabbit had a stubborn and familiar look on her face. PK knew exactly what it meant. It meant that no power on earth could get Rabbit into that bathtub, unless Rabbit *wanted* to get into the tub.

"PK," said Mama, "Rabbit does not want to take her bath—"

"Yes, I *do* want to take my bath," Rabbit said.

"But only if you tell her a story," said Mama. "She's worried because there's no hamper here to get stories out of."

"I know," said PK. "I was worried about that, too. Now I'm not worried anymore."

"You aren't?" asked Rabbit.

"No," said PK. "Now I know where the stories are."

"Where?" asked Rabbit.

"They are still in the old hamper in the old building. But I can get them out long-distance. All I do is open the little window in my mind, and the stories fly into it."

"Wow," Rabbit said. "That is *so* cool." Rabbit looked happy for the first time since they had 84 · moved. She relaxed her arm-branches.

"Well," Mama said. "I guess Rabbit can take her bath, right?"

"Yes," said Rabbit. She got into the tub. She wet her washrag in the running water. Instead of sucking it, she stuck her lower lip out and blew air up. Rabbit had finally fluttered her bangs. It was easy.

"I am ready," she said, and fluttered her bangs again beautifully.

"Mama," said PK. "I need to sit there, please."

Mama had been sitting on the lid of the toilet. "Okay," she said. She sat down in the middle of the floor, looking a little puzzled.

PK got into position on the toilet-seat lid. She took off her sandals. She put her feet on the edge and hugged her knees. She curled her toes up. She concentrated on the built-in clothes hamper in the old bathroom.

She almost did not notice when Megan came in and hoisted herself up on the sink.

Pretty soon, a little window in PK's mind opened and a story flew in.

It was a good one.